CREE
WINS THE DAY!

By: Lora Bynum and Ti Dandy
Illustrated by: Jershel Johnson

"We dedicate this book to all the children in our lives who inspired us through their individuality, creativity, and uniqueness.

We also would like to thank our friends and family that supported us and helped to make this dream a reality.

We love you all.

Being yourself is the key to winning!"

- Lora and Ti

Sometimes I wake up and I feel so sad.

I can't find my backpack.

Sometimes I wake up and I feel so mad.

My hair is all over my head.

Sometimes I wake up... Ooops, I wet the bed!

I almost forget my shoes. They are under the bed.

The voices in my head,
they sound so real.

They tell me Fluffy is my only friend,
except when I play pretend.

Shhh...

How do I quiet them down
or put them to an end?

Shhh...

I have so many emotions.
I don't know what to do.

"Cree, let's go!"
Mom yells from below.

"We will be late if you keep
moving so slow."

Today, my brain feels fuzzy wuzzy.
I don't even want to play with my cat, Fluffy.

I'm not sure which feelings are true.
I can't decide what's real. Can you?

Today, I met a new
kid in school named
Penelope.
She asked me why
the other kids never
play with me.

She said she'd be my friend.
She told me to be strong.

But when the teacher
called my name,
Penelope was gone.

I knew I was going to blow up when I walked into the classroom.

The more the teacher talks, the more I try to ignore.

The
teacher
keeps
talking.

The kids
keep
running.

Science,
reading,
and
math...

I'm
feeling
like a
volcano.

I'm
about
to
erupt!

BANG!

I throw my books
on the floor.

BOOM!

I stomp my feet
and slam the door.

Before I know it, I am at the principal's office.

My eyes begin to water. My frustration takes over.
Heavy Breathing, Kicking, Yelling and Screaming!
Everything is a blur, even Principal Stephens.

She tries to calm me,
but it doesn't help.

Even her gentle voice
makes me go berserk!

FLOP!

I sit down
in the counselor's office.

Unlike the principal,
Mr. Brooks says
I'm not having a fit.

That's why he's my #1 pick.

He shows me ways to make new friends.

"Don't be shy. Walk up with a friendly smile and just say, 'Hi!'"

When I'm upset and have no clue about what to do,

I'll take a breath and press reset, or count

1, 2, 3...

'Whew', that really helps me!

He says that I am awesome and smart.

Now I know that there are many kids just like me.

I am amazing, and I should never doubt my abilities.

Now, I'll be sure to talk to those who support me:

my teachers,
counselors,
and parents.

So happy to be home where I can be free!

It was such a rough day.

Mom, Dad, and Fluffy, we are all going to play.

Tomorrow will be better; just you wait and see,

because my difference is not a disAbility.

It's
my
ability
to
simply
be

Me!

www.ingramcontent.com/pod-product-compliance
Lightning Source LLC
Chambersburg PA
CBHW041544240626
47164CB00002B/121